Eggs Over Easy

Eggs Over Easy

• Katharine Kenah •

illustrated by Maxie Chambliss

Dutton Children's Books
New York

Library of Congress Cataloging-in-Publication Data
Kenah, Katharine.
Eggs over easy / by Katharine Kenah; illustrated by Maxie Chambliss.
1st ed.   p.   cm.
Summary: When Sam cares for some abandoned duck eggs, he learns
something about his father, who moved out but still writes him weekly.
ISBN 0-525-45071-8
[1. Ducks—Fiction.   2. Fathers and sons—Fiction.   3. Eggs—Fiction.]
I. Chambliss, Maxie, ill.   II. Title.
PZ7.K315Eg   1993   [Fic]—dc20   93-13254   CIP   AC

Published in the United States by
Dutton Children's Books,
a division of Penguin Books USA Inc.
375 Hudson Street, New York, New York 10014
Designed by Carolyn Boschi
Printed in U.S.A.
First Edition
1 3 5 7 9 10 8 6 4 2

For my own brood—
Eben, Hannah, and Molly—
and for Wilkie, with love
K.K.

To Harold Essigmann,
with love and thanks
M.C.

· CONTENTS ·

Eggs Over Easy

GONE!

Where is she? What *happened?* Sam Jessop thought of a dozen answers to these questions as he raced along the sidewalk. None of them were good. Sam slid to a stop outside the old brick apartment building and tossed his bicycle down. The handlebar caught the bag he was carrying and ripped it open.

Bread crumbs rained over the ground. "What *next?*" Sam asked himself.

As he scooped up the bread, the contents of

his backpack fell out. A sketch pad and pencils tumbled past his shoulders and hit the cement.

"Who needs this stuff anyway?" Sam kicked the sketch pad under a hedge by the front step. Besides, what was the use? It was too late now to draw her—*or* feed her. She was gone! Sam stuffed the torn bag into his jacket and bolted up the steps into the building.

The fourth-floor hallway was deserted when he pounded on the door of apartment 4B.

"Open up, Rowen," Sam called. "It's me." Sam knocked so loudly that he expected doors to fly back all along the silent hall. But only one door inched backward. A pair of binoculars emerged in the opening.

"Stop spying, Howard. I know it's you," Sam said.

Howard's door closed, and Sam rested his head against 4B. He held his breath, trying to slow the pounding in his chest. Please, *be* there, Sam thought. "Rowen, she's gone!"

The door opened suddenly. "It *is* you. I wasn't sure I heard anything," said Rowen Doyle. "My grandfather's got the radio on full blast."

4

"She's gone," Sam repeated.

"Who's gone?"

"Our *duck*. Something's wrong—I know it."

"No way," Rowen said calmly. "She was fine when we fed her yesterday." He brushed a freckled hand through his red hair. "Bet she just went for a walk or something. I would, if all I had to do was sit on a bunch of eggs all day."

"You're *wrong*." Sam's voice rose. "She's been sitting there for weeks. She wouldn't leave her eggs now." Sam grabbed Rowen's arm. "It's bad. I can feel it in my bones."

Rowen grinned. "Your bones have been wrong before."

"Not this time," Sam said quietly. He turned quickly and walked down the hall toward the elevator.

"Where are you going?" Rowen called.

"To get a bucket."

"What for?"

"The *eggs*," Sam hollered. "I'm not leaving them all alone in the park. A dog could get them, or a kid might steal them."

"Hey, wait for me." Rowen slammed his apart-

5

ment door and followed Sam down the hall. He poked the elevator call button on the wall. A rumbling started in the elevator shaft.

"Come on, come on," Sam mumbled, watching the triangular light above the doors. "Why does this elevator take so long? We've got to get back to the park before the eggs get cold."

When the elevator doors slid open, the boys saw the building superintendent inside, holding a vacuum cleaner. He wore a slate-blue work suit, leather boots, and a ring of jingling keys on a belt around his broad middle. He squinted at Sam and Rowen.

"I was hoping to catch up with you two," he said. Mr. Hedges pointed the vacuum hose at them. "Someone's been tracking mud and grass through the lobby lately—and today I found *bread crumbs*. Know anything about it?"

Sam jammed a fist into his jacket to squash the bag bulging from his pocket.

Rowen smiled broadly at Mr. Hedges. "We'll keep an eye out for anyone suspicious."

They backed away from Mr. Hedges and the el-

evator, and pushed through the door of the fire exit. Inside the stairwell, Sam glanced at Rowen and rolled his eyes. They clattered down the stairs to the second floor, two steps at a time.

"Hey, Sam," Rowen said. "Maybe you checked the wrong nest this morning. There are so many nests around the lake now, it would be easy to get mixed up."

Sam wheeled around. "Are you nuts? Of course it was the right one!" His eyes flashed. "It was our nest, and the mother duck's gone." Sam swallowed. Like my father, he thought. He remembered clearly the day his father had moved out a year ago. "*I'm* not going to leave those eggs."

Without another word, they raced to the end of the hall.

"It's us," Sam called, banging on the door with his fist. "Rachel, Rosy, open up."

The door of apartment 2H moved a few inches. Two green-eyed four-year-olds peeked through the slit.

Rowen and Sam pushed their way in. "Want a

haircut?" Rachel asked. She was holding a pair of fingernail scissors.

Sam covered his hair with his hands. "Aaagh, get *away* from me!" he said. "Where's Mrs. Perch?"

Rachel pointed to the kitchen. "On the phone."

"Not again! Mom might as well have hired a puppy to baby-sit for the twins. Mrs. Perch is *always* on the phone." He tossed his backpack onto the cluttered couch.

Rosy stood on Rowen's feet and grabbed his hands. "Dance me," she said.

"Can't today." Rowen shook his feet loose. "We're in a hurry. We have to get a bucket."

"Why?" Rosy frowned.

"Never mind," Rowen said. He made a face at Rosy, and she beamed at him.

"You can't have it," said Rachel. She put her small hands on her hips. "Theodore and Freddie are swimming in it."

Sam headed straight for the bathroom. Two dolls were sticking out of a bucket in the bathtub. The dolls' hair had been cut into stalks that stuck up like nailbrushes from their pink plastic scalps.

Rowen whistled. "Nice haircuts!"

Sam threw the dripping dolls onto towels. "Sorry, guys," he said, emptying the bucket. "This is an emergency. Theodore and Freddie can swim tomorrow. We need the bucket now."

"What's a *'mergency?*" Rachel asked.

"Nothing." Sam glanced at Rowen and then at the twins. "Tell Mrs. Perch I'll be back . . . later. On second thought, don't tell her anything." He pulled Rowen toward the door. "Let's go."

"See ya, guys," Rowen called. "Don't give any more haircuts while we're gone."

2

ALL ALONE

"Look at this crowd," Sam said to Rowen when they were two blocks from their building. "If the park's this busy, someone might step on the eggs or smash them with a ball before we get there."

Saturday shoppers jammed the sidewalk. Parents pushed strollers. Dogs tugged at leashes. Joggers loped along the bike path across the street, heading for the park. Sam held the bucket tightly as they hurried along.

"Maybe we could get another duck to sit on the nest," Rowen said. He had to run to keep up. "Or maybe the father duck will come back and take care of them."

"Fathers! Are you kidding? That duck wasn't paying any attention this morning." Sam waved the bucket angrily. "He's probably floating around by the popcorn stand, showing off his shiny green head, while his kids are all bald and exposed. He's just like my father—*gone.*"

"You're not being fair," Rowen said slowly, "and you know it. Your father writes to you every week, and you don't even *read* his letters."

Sam looked away.

They crossed the street and raced by the Fourth National Bank and the beauty shop. Rowen stopped suddenly in front of the bakery.

"Mom's working today," Sam whispered, nodding toward the glass. He hid the bucket behind his back. "Wave or she'll wonder what we're up to."

They waved and smiled at Mrs. Jessop inside the bakery. When she waved back, Rowen stuck out his tongue and clutched his chest like a dying man, pointing to the pastries in the window. Sam's mother laughed and turned back to the cupcakes she was frosting.

"Cut it out. We don't have time to goof around," said Sam. "The eggs are getting cold."

They hurried past the shops and then sprinted as they neared the park. Sam and Rowen bolted through the brick gates. They ran down the long slope to the lake. The shore was shaggy with willow trees and overgrown grass.

Sam parted the reeds and pointed to a nest made of twigs and soft feathers. "See," he whispered. "What'd I tell you?"

Inside, alone and unprotected, were eight pale ivory-colored eggs. The grass around the nest was trampled. There were paw prints in the dirt. A feather stuck out of the mud at the water's edge.

Rowen let out a long whistle. "You didn't tell me it looked like this! All trampled and messed up. *Why* didn't you tell me? It looks like a dog got her."

"Yeah," Sam murmured. He bit his lip, trying to fight back the tears he felt coming. Kneeling, Sam touched the eggs gently. "They're still warm. We've got to hurry and get them out of here."

Quickly the boys collected handfuls of grass and dropped them into the bucket. Then, one by one, they lifted the eggs from the nest and placed them carefully onto the soft green bedding.

Sam stripped off his jacket and tucked it over the eggs. "Okay," he said. "Let's go."

"Where?"

"Home." Clutching the bucket, Sam hurried up the grassy slope toward the park gates.

"Then what?" Rowen called. He followed Sam across the street. "What are we going to *do* with them? Do you know how warm they have to be —or how long it takes them to hatch?"

"I thought *you* knew." Sam rested the heavy bucket on a wooden bench. "Hey! We hatched chick eggs in first grade—remember? Duck hatching can't be that different. I think we should go to the library and get some books. We can't let the eggs die."

Rowen slowly followed Sam. "The eggs aren't the only ones in trouble. Wait till the librarian sees me. My book on comets must be fifty-three days overdue!"

3

REGULAR
DUCKS

"Look out," said Rowen. "I see Emily."

Emily Trimble, a sixth grader from their building, was coming out of the library as the boys arrived. "Hey, Sam," she called. "What's in there?"

Sam slid the bucket behind his back. "Don't ask," he said. "You don't want to know."

"Why not? What is it?" she asked.

"A snake," Rowen whispered. "We're going to build a reptile habitat to surprise his mother."

"She'll be *surprised,* all right," Emily said, wrinkling her nose. She hurried down the steps past the boys. From a safe distance, Emily turned around and yelled, "They'll never let you into the library with that bucket." Then she ran off.

Sam stared at Rowen. "She's right! We can't take the eggs in there. What are we going to do?"

"You go," Rowen answered. "We'll wait here." He took the bucket from Sam. Then he settled himself in the sunshine on the stone steps, next to a statue of a lion. "Go *on.* They'll be fine."

Sam hesitated, then ran up the steps. Inside, the library was dim. He stood still and blinked while his eyes adjusted. Two small boys splashed each other at a water fountain. No one was at the information desk.

"May I help you?" someone asked.

Sam turned and saw the librarian stapling a poster to the wall. "Uh . . . yes, thanks," Sam stammered. "I need to find out about hatching eggs."

"Eggs," the librarian said. "What kind of eggs?"

"Duck," Sam whispered, glancing around. He

coughed and blushed slowly. "It's for . . . a . . . science project."

"What kind of ducks are you studying?"

"Just regular ones . . . like the ducks at the park."

"Regular, huh?" said the librarian. "Ducks would be under nonfiction. Let's go check the card catalog."

In the brightly lit reference room, the librarian said, "I'll look up *ducks*. You find *incubators* in the encyclopedia."

"Sure," said Sam. He crossed the room and pulled the *I* volume from a set of red books. "*Incubator* . . . *i-n-q* . . . No, no . . . *i-n-c*," he spelled aloud. Sam turned the pages rapidly. "Here it is!"

" 'Most incubators maintain a constant temperature of 99.5 to 100 degrees,' " he read. Sam thought about the eggs in the bucket. What if they weren't that warm by now? What if they *died* before he knew how to hatch them? Sam's stomach started to fall as if he were in an elevator.

"Any luck?" The librarian appeared beside Sam with a book and started to read. " 'A female mallard builds a shallow nest from twigs and dry grass. She makes it soft and warm with feathers plucked from her chest.' "

"I know," Sam said softly, leaning over to study the photo of a nesting mallard at the top of the page. "I've seen a nest like that."

The librarian continued. " 'The mother duck rolls the eggs over with her beak several times each day to keep them evenly warm. Incubation time is twenty-eight days.' "

"Twenty-eight days," Sam echoed. "Thanks!"

In ten minutes, he had the information he needed. Sam tiptoed through the reading room and dashed outdoors.

Rowen was waiting on the steps. His face was red from the sun.

"Rowen, I've got it. I know what to do," Sam called. "The eggs have to stay at one hundred degrees and be kept in moist air and be turned every few hours—" Sam grabbed Rowen's arm. "*Where's* the bucket?" he asked.

Rowen pointed to the stone lion behind him. Hidden safely between its back feet was the bucket, warm in the sun and out of sight.

"You're crazy!" Sam grinned and reached for the eggs.

4

CAT-FOOD CANS

Back in the lobby of their building, Sam and Rowen pounded the elevator call button. Finally the bell dinged, and the doors slid open. Inside was Howard Gunderson with binoculars dangling from his neck.

"Oh, no," groaned Sam.

"Well, if it isn't the fourth-floor spy," Rowen said. He hurried into the elevator. "Get out, Howard."

Howard did not move. "What's in the bucket?" he asked.

"We can't tell you," Rowen said. "You're too young to know."

"What is it really?" Howard whispered. "I won't tell anyone."

"Germs," Sam said. "Live germs." He stepped into the elevator and pushed the button for the fourth floor. "We're conducting a scientific experiment on contagious diseases."

Howard backed into the corner and covered his binoculars with his hands. The instant the elevator reached the fourth floor, he shot through the doors and ran down the hall.

Rowen stood still.

"Aren't you getting out?" Sam asked. "We have to hide the eggs in your apartment."

"We can't put them in *my* apartment," Rowen said. "You know what my parents are like. They go crazy if my fish lets his food drift on the water too long." He stared at Sam. "I thought we were going to *your* apartment. Your mom doesn't mind messy stuff."

Sam gulped. His mouth felt like cotton. "My apartment won't work. Rosy and Rachel find everything."

"So what are we going to do?" Rowen said. "We can't leave them in our apartments. We can't take them to school. And Mr. Hedges doesn't allow pets in the building—except for his rotten cat. This will never work."

"Yes it will," Sam said fiercely. "You're wrong. We can do it. We *have* to. We'll hide them on the roof."

"Too cold—and wet, if it rains," Rowen said.

"Then we'll put them in the laundry room."

"Too many people."

Sam put his hand under the jacket and touched the eggs. He felt frantic. "They're almost cool!" He reached around Rowen and pushed the bottom button. "The basement is the only place."

"Are you *nuts?*" Rowen asked. "You know we're not allowed anywhere down there except the laundry room."

"Mr. Hedges won't find out." Sam pointed to his watch. "It's twelve-forty. He won't be back from lunch for another twenty minutes."

The superintendent left at noon each day. With the exactness of a clock, he returned at 1:00.

"We'll find a good place for them if it's the last thing we do!" Sam said.

Rowen groaned and closed his eyes as the elevator plunged downward. *"Don't* say that."

The elevator doors opened onto a wide passageway that smelled of soap, oil, and damp cement. To the right was the bright laundry room. Washing machines and dryers stood in green rows beneath a huge television. To the left, the passageway was dark and musty. A hand-carved sign, HAROLD HEDGES—PRIVATE, hung on the first door. Farther along the hall was the broom closet, where a faucet dripped steadily into a chipped enamel sink.

"Look for someplace warm and moist," said Sam. "The library books said the eggs should be kept around one hundred degrees."

Rowen licked his finger and held it up, testing the air. "Now *how* are we supposed to tell when someplace is one hundred degrees?"

Sam hugged the bucket, looking around. "I guess it would feel like a person with a fever."

But no place felt like a fever. The floor was cold. The broom closet was damp and ripe with the smell of old mops. Sam stepped inside and climbed a ladder to check the shelf above the sink.

"No place warm up here," he mumbled. "Just sponges, soap, paper towels, and cans for recycling." Sam's hand knocked over a stack of empty cat-food cans that clattered to the floor.

"Jeeez!" Rowen said. "You want everyone in the whole building to know we're down here?"

Sam hopped down to collect the cans and jumped back in surprise. Two golden eyes were watching him warily from a box under the sink. It was Mr. Hedges' scrawny cat, Morton.

"This place gives me the creeps," said Rowen. He tapped Sam on the back and cackled a monster laugh that echoed through the passageway.

"Don't do that! Someone will come looking for the weirdo in the basement." Sam pointed to the cat. "The broom closet is definitely not the place."

Rowen explored the deserted laundry room. "Maybe we could hide the bucket behind the dryers," he suggested. "Bet it gets warm back there when the machines are on."

Sam followed him into the laundry room with the bucket. "But it gets crowded. Someone's bound to spot—"

PFssT . . . FFZZZ

"What was that?" Rowen looked around quickly.

A loud hissing sound came from a dark open doorway behind the row of washing machines.

Pfsss . . . SSS

Sam's hands turned clammy. He rubbed them hard against his shirt and wished he and Rowen had looked for a hiding place on the roof. "Whatever it is, it's in there," he whispered, nodding toward the door.

"It's probably nothing," Rowen said. "Who would hang around in a place like that?" His voice wavered.

Sam clutched the bucket tightly as they inched along the wall. Near the doorway, a cloud of warm air drifted over them.

"Go ahead," Rowen whispered.

Sam reached through the dark and flicked a switch. Suddenly the room was ablaze with light.

PPSssFFFT . . . SSssFFT

"See," Rowen said, taking a deep breath. "It's only the boiler. I knew it all along."

"You did not!" retorted Sam.

Sam felt triumphant. Ever since second grade, Rowen had been first—to grow tall, to finish reports, to understand insect flight. But now Rowen wasn't sure what to do. Sam smiled at his best friend and edged through the door—first.

An old steel boiler hissed and gurgled in front of them. It heated the building in the winter. But now, in warmer weather, it heated water for the apartments above. It looked like a gigantic loaf of bread—nine feet tall and six feet wide.

"Hey!" Sam said suddenly. He held out his hand. "Feel that?"

"Feel what?" asked Rowen.

"This room. It feels like a fever!"

Rowen squinted up at the greasy glass thermometer jutting from the side of the boiler. "It says *one hundred degrees.*"

Sam shot his fist joyfully into the air. "Hot dog! I knew it!" he said. "It's perfect for the eggs."

"Yeah, but where are we going to put the bucket?" Rowen waved his hand at the boiler. "It'll never fit under that thing. Besides, Mr. Hedges will spot it."

"The top," Sam said. "It's the only place."

"The eggs will roll off."

"Want to bet? I've got an idea."

Sam handed the bucket to Rowen and raced to the broom closet. In a flash, he was up the ladder and loading his arms with empty cat-food cans. One can dropped to the floor beside Morton's box. The cat jumped and retreated in a huff to the laundry room.

"What are you doing with those cans?" Rowen asked.

"I'm going to make nests—you'll see."

"Well, *hurry up,*" Rowen said. He glanced at the clock on the wall. "It's almost one o'clock. Mr. Hedges will be back from lunch any minute."

Sam lifted a handful of grass from the bucket

and patted it around the inside of a can. Rowen watched, then grabbed a can and made a second nest. When eight cans were ready, they tucked an egg into each one and carried them to the boiler. Sam dragged the ladder from the broom closet. He propped it against the boiler and climbed to the top.

"Hurry up," Rowen warned again.

"All right, already!" Sam blew dust and dead flies from the warm, flat top of the boiler. Rowen passed the cans up. Sam set them carefully in a cluster at the center.

"That's good," Rowen said. "I can't see them at all from down here."

Morton came slinking into the boiler room. He circled Rowen's ankles and rubbed his whiskers on the bottom rung of the ladder.

"Get out of here, Morton," Sam said. He hopped to the floor and shooed the cat ahead of them. Then they carried the ladder back to the broom closet.

The moment it slid into place, they heard the rumbling sounds of the elevator.

"Oh, *great,*" Rowen yelped. "Mr. Hedges is back."

"Hit the stairs!" Sam cried.

They dove through the fire exit and thundered up the metal steps as the elevator doors opened in the basement.

• 5 •

GOOD
RIDDANCE

Sam collapsed on the second-floor landing, gasping. "We . . . did it. We did it!" he exclaimed. "The eggs are safe."

"Not yet," Rowen said. He sat on the empty bucket. "What about *turning* the eggs every few hours and keeping them *moist*—all that stuff you told me at the library. It was dry and dusty in the boiler room."

"Shoot!" Sam groaned. How could he have forgotten so soon? All that work, and the eggs still weren't safe. Sam rubbed his eyes wearily. "How could I be so *dumb?*" His voice echoed in the stairwell.

"Don't yell—someone will hear us." Rowen leaned forward and whispered, "I don't think we can hatch those eggs without help. Maybe my grandfather could check on them while we're at school. He watches all the wildlife shows on television."

Sam shot to his feet. "No—never. You can't tell him, or anyone. Promise! He might tell Mr. Hedges by accident, and if *he* finds out, you know what will happen."

"You're not being practical." Rowen thumped Sam lightly with his fist. "How can we turn the eggs and keep Mr. Hedges out of the basement— so he doesn't kill us when he finds out—and go to school all at the same time? It'll be too hard to manage with just the two of us."

"We can do it," Sam pleaded. "I *know* we can. We've got all the information from the library. We don't need anyone else."

"Mr. Hedges is already suspicious of us."

Rowen looked away from Sam without speaking for a moment. "Listen," he said finally. "I think we should take the eggs back to the park. I don't want to get thrown out of the building for this."

"Fine! I don't need your help." Sam's face turned deep red. "I don't *want* your help. I can take care of the eggs alone."

"Good luck," said Rowen. "You're on your own." He tossed the empty bucket to Sam and dashed up the steps. The stairwell rumbled, then grew still. Sam heard the door bang shut on the fourth floor.

"Good riddance," he whispered without moving. Sam wished he could take back his words. He wanted Rowen to come back. But he would *never* take the eggs back to the park.

The lobby was busy that afternoon with the usual Saturday traffic. Sam sat on a planter by the elevator. He was holding a laundry basket.

"Going up, Sam?" asked Kasie Cassetta, Sam's neighbor. She was in seventh grade and a whole foot taller than Sam.

"Nope." Sam shook his head. "I'm busy."

"Since when do you do laundry?" asked Kasie. "You sick or something?"

"Very funny." Sam set the basket by the ferns and stood up. "Hey, Kasie, have you seen Mr. Hedges?"

"Sure," she said. "He's on our floor—trying to pop the balloons some idiot shoved into the mail chute. Stay out of his way. He's *really* steamed." She stepped into the elevator, and the doors closed.

Hope they can't fingerprint balloons, Sam thought, rubbing his forehead. He had turned the eggs once that afternoon. But night was coming. The thought of being alone in the basement at night made Sam's stomach twist like a pretzel. He closed his eyes and moaned.

"Are you sick or something?"

Sam opened his eyes. Howard stood ten inches away, staring at him through binoculars. He was wearing a green-and-brown camouflage suit and boots.

"Jeeez, Howard!" Sam jumped back. "Don't sneak up on people like that."

Howard glanced around the lobby, then leaned

close to Sam. "I saw you unscrewing light bulbs on our floor," he whispered. "And I *know* you put the balloons in the mail chute."

"Go away, Howard."

"I've been watching you. You're doing weird stuff all over the building. You even did laundry!" Howard squinted at him. "I bet it's got something to do with that bucket of germs you and Rowen had in the elevator this morning. If I catch anything, I'm telling."

Sam grabbed Howard's binoculars and pulled him close. "Don't you tell *anyone* about that bucket!"

"Okay." Howard sniffed and pulled his binoculars back. "Let go . . . please."

Sam released him slowly. Darn midget spy, Sam thought. Howard was truly amazing. He could spot an ant a mile away. Suddenly Sam took a deep breath. Spy! Howard was *perfect*. "Hey, Howard, you're really brave, right? And smart? Want to go on a secret mission with me tonight?"

Howard nodded, eyes wide.

"Good," Sam said. "Ask your mother if you can stay at my apartment tonight. Bring your sleeping bag over after supper."

"*Really?* You mean it?" Howard's eyebrows rose like umbrellas.

"Yeah."

"Hot dog!" Howard dashed away. "Thanks, Sam!" he shouted. "I won't tell anyone . . . I promi—"

The elevator swallowed his final word.

"Hope he likes basements," Sam murmured.

During supper that evening, Sam poked the fluffy omelette on his plate. The thought of eating eggs made him lose his appetite. He made small mounds of the mushrooms, tomatoes, and onions. But he couldn't keep his mind off the eggs in the basement. He tried not to worry about turning them that night. After all, it might be easier than turning them during the day. Mr. Hedges would be asleep. *Probably.* And so would Rowen—that rat! And Sam would have Howard-the-Spy.

"Sam!" Mrs. Jessop interrupted his thoughts. "Are you all right?"

"Sure, Mom."

"Then why aren't you eating?"

Sam put his fork down. "Guess I'm not hungry."

"You're worn out," his mother said. "It's no wonder. You were off in a hundred directions today. Thanks for doing laundry this afternoon."

"No big deal," Sam mumbled.

Rachel looked up, with solemn eyes and a milk mustache. She turned to her mother. "Sam had a 'mergency today."

Rosy nodded. "Theodore and Freddie had to stop swimming."

Mrs. Jessop glanced at Sam. "While I was at work? What happened?"

"Nothing," Sam said quickly. He shifted uneasily in his chair. "Rowen and I went to the park this morning, that's all . . . with that leftover bread you brought from the bakery. The ducks gobbled it all." He grabbed a warm cinnamon roll from his plate and took a huge bite.

Rosy frowned at Sam. "Why does Sam get to have company tonight? Can we have somebody?"

"Howard's not company," announced Rachel. "He's just—"

"A neighbor . . . and *welcome* anytime." Mrs. Jessop eyed her sternly. "Sam . . ." She hesitated. "Sam, you got another letter from your father today."

Mrs. Jessop pulled a blue envelope from the pocket of her jeans and laid it beside his plate.

Sam choked suddenly and rose, coughing. "May . . . I . . . be excused?" He pounded his chest. Before his mother could answer, Sam left the kitchen. He did not touch the letter.

6

NIGHT NOISES

By midnight that night, Howard had consumed three cans of soda, a package of cookies, and half a bag of potato chips. He was wide awake and whispering on the floor of Sam's bedroom.

"Why didn't you tell me you had *eggs* in the bucket? You were just kidding about that contagious disease stuff—right? Anyway, I got it figured out. We hang a net across the top of the elevator and send it down to the basement with an alarm clock ready to buzz. Mr. Hedges wakes up, steps into the elevator to see what's happening, and he's trapped! He'll toss and turn—"

Howard demonstrated from his sleeping bag, arms flailing like a fish in a net. "Then we rush up the ladder and turn the eggs. No problem!"

"While everyone in the building *and* the police catch us, after Mr. Hedges sets off every alarm in the place." Sam was sitting up in bed, fully dressed. "Howard," he explained for the fourth time. "We can't let anyone know what we're doing. If someone finds out, they might get rid of the eggs."

"Bet they wouldn't," Howard said.

Sam lunged over the side of the bed and grabbed the sleeve of Howard's Superman pajamas. "The eggs are *secret.* Understand? Now go to sleep."

"Sure . . . okay!" Howard picked up his binoculars and scanned Sam's room. He zoomed past the clipper-ship wallpaper, over the microscope and magazines on the desk, and focused on the bookcase. "Why are all those blue envelopes stuck between the books?"

"No reason. Never mind. Just forget them."
They're none of your business, Sam thought.
They don't mean *anything.*

Sam jumped out of bed and snatched the letters from the bookcase. He tossed them into the wastebasket. "Go to sleep, will you? I'll wake you up when it's safe to go."

"Yeah. Okay, Sam . . . sure."

Howard drifted to sleep without another word. When his breathing was steady, Sam crept across the room. He fished the letters from the wastebasket and dropped them into his dresser drawer. In bed again, Sam fell asleep, waiting for the building to grow silent.

The alarm clock went off beside Sam's ear just past two o'clock. He sat up listening. The building was still. The light beneath his mother's bedroom door was gone. Sam poked Howard. "Get up," he whispered.

Howard snorted and rolled over. In his sleeping bag, he looked like a red nylon caterpillar. Sam poked him again. Howard sat up, rubbing his ears, and reached for his boots.

"Leave them here." Sam nodded toward the boots. "They'll make too much noise." He pulled a flashlight from his pillowcase and switched it on.

Without speaking, they moved through the apartment. The living room was a maze of furniture and scattered dolls.

"Careful," Howard whispered, as Sam reached for the chain lock on the front door. "Those things are noisy."

Sam laid the chain silently against the door. He held his breath and pulled the door backward about an inch a century. Finally, they stepped into the hall. "Made it!" Sam exclaimed.

Someone laughed faintly behind a closed door down the hall.

Howard froze. "Maybe we should go back," he said. His eyes looked as round as plates.

"We *can't*." Sam swallowed. His mouth was dry. His heart hammered in his chest. "The eggs have to be turned. If we don't do it tonight, the ducklings might stick to their shells and never hatch."

"Can't you do it yourself . . . like you did this afternoon?" Howard pleaded. "Why do I have to go?"

"Because Mr. Hedges turns the basement lights off at night, and I can't turn them on without being spotted. You have to hold the flashlight and stand guard, so I can turn the eggs." Please, Sam thought, don't chicken out on me now. "Come on, it'll be fine." He smiled encouragingly. "You're a good spy—right?"

Howard nodded weakly and held up the binoculars dangling from his neck.

"See?" Sam whispered. "Ready for action!" He tried to look eager and brave, but he felt miserable. What if Mr. Hedges heard them? What if the ladder was gone? Sam wished he could trade Howard for Rowen. He made himself push open the door to the fire exit. Inside the stairwell, the lights were blazing.

"I'll stand guard right here," Howard croaked.

"Howard!"

They padded silently down the metal steps. At the bottom of the stairs was a large yellow door with a stenciled sign: FIRE DOOR—KEEP CLOSED AT ALL TIMES.

"It's locked. Too bad," Howard said, turning around instantly. "We'd better go back to your apartment."

"Howard," Sam warned again, then put a finger to his lips. He pulled on the heavy door, and it opened with ease. It wasn't locked.

After the glare of the stairwell, the basement was as black as a cave. Sam shone the flashlight over the walls—past the elevator, past Mr. Hedges' apartment. They followed the beam to the broom closet.

The steady *plink, plink* of the dripping faucet seemed loud in the dark. Sam handed the flashlight to Howard and walked over to pick up the ladder. He carried it down the passageway to the laundry room. "The boiler room is through that door in back of the washing machines," Sam whispered.

Behind him, Howard aimed a wobbling beam of light over the raised lids of the washing machines.

"Howard!" Sam hissed. "Point that thing so I

can see where I'm going! I nearly rammed the dryers with the ladder. You want Mr. Hedges to wake up?"

It seemed to take forever for Howard to creep into the boiler room ahead of Sam.

"Go on, go *on,*" Sam urged. "Hurry."

In moments, Sam propped the ladder against the side of the boiler and then climbed to the top. One by one, he turned each egg, fluffing the grass in the cat-food-can nests with his fingertip.

"Why'd you put them up there?" Howard asked, straining on tiptoe for a better view. "I can't see anything." He held the flashlight up with both hands.

" 'Cause it's warm," Sam said, "and high, and no one can see them." He patted the side of the boiler. "And the top of the boiler is the same temperature as an incub—" Sam stopped talking.

"What's the matter?"

"The boiler isn't as warm as it was before . . . and it's quiet!" Sam whispered. "I *knew* something was different. It should be gurgling and hissing." He looked down at Howard. "Do you see any knobs or switches down there?"

Howard surveyed the bottom of the boiler with the flashlight. "Nope," he said.

"Darn." Sam wanted to give the boiler a swift kick, but Mr. Hedges could probably hear through concrete. "What's *wrong* with this darn thing?"

"No one's taking a bath," said Howard.

"So?"

"If no one's using hot water, the boiler doesn't come on."

"That's right! Howard, you're a genius." Sam came down the ladder so fast he almost fell. "We've got to get back upstairs. We've got to turn on all the hot water faucets. If the boiler doesn't start up soon, the eggs will *die.*"

They followed Howard's wavering circle of light down the passageway and shoved the ladder into the broom closet.

MreooooOW . . . AaoooOW!

A screech filled the passageway.

Howard flattened against the wall. With shaking hands, Sam grabbed the flashlight and aimed straight down. Two cat eyes flashed in the light. The ladder had landed on Morton's scraggly tail.

"I'm coming—I'm coming," Mr. Hedges called from his apartment. "Worthless cat. Why don't you go out *before* I go to bed?"

"He's awake!" Howard clutched the sink, trembling.

"Go—*now*, before he opens his door," Sam ordered.

Silently they padded past Mr. Hedges' door, then bolted through the fire exit.

They raced up two flights of stairs before Howard stopped suddenly. "I can't . . . breathe," he gasped.

"Keep going, *don't* stop." Sam dragged Howard to his feet. "We have to get upstairs. We have to turn on the hot water. We have to get the boiler going before the eggs cool—"

"What's this *we* stuff?" Howard wailed. "I'm not going anywhere with you again."

7

UPSTAIRS, DOWNSTAIRS

The next morning, Sam deposited Howard and his sleeping bag on the fourth floor. Then he went down to buy the Sunday newspaper for his mother. He dropped coins into the vending machine and opened the door. Mr. Hedges was crossing the lobby with a carton of small empty cans. It *couldn't* be—Sam shut out the terrible thought.

"Mr. Hedges," Sam called, trying to sound calm. "What have you got?"

"Cans for recycling." Mr. Hedges shifted the box in his arms. "I'm taking them out to the crusher."

"Cru . . . cru . . ." Sam swallowed. "You're going to *squash* them?"

"Same as always. What's the matter with you?"

"Where'd you get those cans?" Sam asked, barely breathing.

"The basement."

Whump! Sam let go of the vending-machine door. It locked shut, eating his quarters before he'd reached for the newspaper.

Mr. Hedges shook his head and moved down the hallway toward the back of the building.

Sam watched him go, hesitated, then started across the lobby. "Mr. Hedges . . . wait!"

Suddenly Rowen stepped around the corner from the mailboxes. "They're fine," he said, and crossed over to Sam.

"What?" Sam asked, startled.

Rowen looked straight at him. "The eggs are *fine*," he said quietly. "I heard Mr. Hedges out in the alley doing his recycling. So I snuck down to the basement to turn them. The eggs are all on the boiler, warm and safe."

Sam could feel the air sliding into his lungs. It felt like his first breath in hours. "Thanks . . . Rowen."

They stood in silence for a moment. Then Rowen punched the vending machine. "I saw what happened," he said, grinning at Sam. "Nice move. Hope you've got more quarters."

Sam looked down as he dug into his pockets. "Hey, Rowen," he said softly. "You were right about needing help. Turning the eggs is harder than I thought. It's too hard for *two* people. I shouldn't have . . . I'm . . . sorry." He dropped more coins into the machine.

"Me, too," said Rowen. He stooped grandly and opened the glass door, while Sam reached for the newspaper.

On Monday evening, Emily sat drumming her cranberry-colored fingernails on Sam's kitchen table. "I still don't get it," she said. "What does hot water have to do with eggs?"

Kasie rolled her eyes. "Tell her again, Sam, but hurry up. I told your mother we were planning a birthday surprise for my brother."

Sam explained again. "Rowen and I watched a duck in the park. She had eggs in a nest. We fed her . . ." He paused, running his thumb along the chipped edge of the table. No matter how many times he said it, it still hurt to remember. "But she vanished. We couldn't just leave the eggs there, so we brought them home in a bucket and put them on the boiler—"

"You sneak!" Emily exclaimed. "You didn't have any snake at the library."

"How long till they hatch?" Kasie asked.

"A week," Sam said. "It *can't* be more than that. The library books said it takes duck eggs four weeks to hatch, and our eggs must be three weeks old already."

"So what exactly are *we* supposed to do?" Emily looked confused.

"Keep Mr. Hedges upstairs when we need you to," Sam said, "so Rowen and I can sneak downstairs to turn the eggs. And use *tons* of hot water, so the boiler stays on and keeps them warm."

The door swung open and Rowen stepped into the kitchen, with Howard following. Sam handed them each a cupcake from a bakery box on the table.

"Can we see the eggs?" Emily asked.

"No . . . no!" Sam shook his head. "If we're all sneaking up and down to the basement, Mr. Hedges will suspect something for sure." He glanced at Rowen. "We *can't* let that happen."

"Well, I'll do more dishes," said Kasie, "and keep the faucets dripping in my apartment." She laughed and poked Emily across the table. "And you just keep doing what you love best. Wash your gorgeous hair four times a day."

Emily groaned.

"I know!" Howard's eyes were shining. "We kidnap Morton and leave notes *all* over the building. Mr. Hedges will look everywhere—"

"Come on. Be serious," said Sam. "Will you help—please? The eggs won't hatch unless we turn them. We can't turn them unless you guys keep Mr. Hedges upstairs."

"It'll be easy, really. Eggs over easy!" Rowen chuckled.

The phone rang in the next room. A moment later, Mrs. Jessop opened the kitchen door. "Rowen, that was your grandfather. He said you should come home now." The door swung closed.

"See ya, guys," Rowen said, sliding off the counter.

Kasie stood up. "I've got to go, too. Math quiz tomorrow." She made a face and left.

Emily looked at Sam. "I'll help," she said slowly. "But I don't know why. You'd better promise we won't get caught."

When everyone had gone, Rosy climbed onto Sam's lap. "What does Emily mean? 'Get caught'?"

"Nothing," Sam said. "Do you think Rachel would like a hot bath with pink bubbles?"

"A bath of her very own?"

He nodded.

Rosy's face fell. "What about *me?*"

"You!" Sam opened his eyes wide. "I guess we

can make more bubbles for you." Sam tickled Rosy until she doubled over with giggles.

Emily took four steamy showers over the next two days. "Look at me!" she complained to Sam on Wednesday morning as they rode the elevator down on their way to school. "Even my mother says I look like a prune. I'll *never* be smooth again." She glanced in the mirror at the back of the elevator and winced. "And my hair—it'll be frizzy till I'm fifty."

"Sam's sisters have a toy lamb with hair like yours," Rowen said. "All fuzzy and—"

Emily hit him. But Rowen just laughed.

"Look!" said Howard. He pulled a hammer from his backpack and waved it proudly. "I made every faucet in our apartment leak. All you have to do is wham with this on the bottom part a little bit, and water shoots out."

Sam sighed. How long can this last? he thought. The ducklings *have* to hatch soon. They'd kept Mr. Hedges upstairs or in the elevator all week, fixing light bulbs, leaky faucets, overflowing tubs, and jammed locks—while the eggs stayed warm and hidden in the basement.

The elevator doors slid open at the lobby. Kasie was waiting by the mailboxes. "Boy, did you guys hear the yelling in our apartment this morning? I promised my stupid little brother a quarter for every bath he took. He turned on the water, then decided to watch cartoons. You should see the flood!"

"Well, that takes care of Mr. Hedges," Rowen said. "He'll be upstairs forever."

Sam hurried toward school, wondering who would arrive in their building first—the ducklings or the police.

• 8 •

UNEXPECTED ARRIVALS

It was Sam's turn to rotate the eggs at lunchtime that day. When he got home at noon, the superintendent was standing on the front stoop. Sam tried to dodge into the alley beside the building, but it was too late.

"Forget your lunch?" Mr. Hedges called.

Sam nodded. He slowly approached the stoop.

"Well, watch your step on the second floor. It's still slippery. Had a flood up there this morning."

Guilt burned through Sam like a heat wave. He

shoved his hands deep into the pockets of his jeans. "Okay," Sam mumbled. "I'll be careful . . . thanks."

Mr. Hedges studied Sam for a moment, then clumped down the steps to the sidewalk. "Well, I'm off for lunch."

Sam rode to the basement in the elevator, then dashed to the broom closet for the ladder. Morton followed him down the passageway. The cat moved low to the ground with his tail flicking.

"Go away." Sam pushed the cat away with his foot and carried the ladder to the boiler. In an instant, he was at the top. "How are you guys doing?" he whispered, turning the smooth, warm eggs.

An old peanut-butter jar filled with water was nestled among the cans.

Good for Rowen, Sam thought. The ducklings would have dried up inside their shells without water. Sam had remembered to keep the eggs warm. He'd remembered to turn them, but—

"Rowen was the one who remembered the water," Sam told Morton. "What a friend!" Sam felt lucky. He returned the ladder to the broom closet, patted the cat, and ran all the way back to school.

On Thursday, Sam raced home with Rowen to turn the eggs at noon. Mr. Hedges was out for lunch.

"The eggs felt weird this morning," Sam said as he propped the ladder against the boiler.

"Weird?" asked Rowen.

"Well, off-balance and wobbly." Sam put his foot on the bottom rung. "Hey, Rowen, thanks for putting the water on top of the boiler. I still can't believe I forgot it."

Rowen stared at Sam. "*I* didn't put the water up there. I thought *you* did."

Before Sam could answer, they heard a faint sound. It was different from the familiar hisses and gurgles of the boiler.

Peep, peep.

In a flash, they scrambled up the ladder together. An egg was rocking in one can as a duckling struggled in its shell. The boys watched the duckling whack its beak against the jagged edges of a small hole. Its whole body pulsed with effort. When it paused between pecks, it peeped sadly.

"Look at that!" Sam shrieked.

With a flurry of activity, the duckling made the opening larger. Its head flopped through the hole. Then it lay still with its eyes closed.

"Think he knocked himself out?" asked Rowen.

Sam shook his head. "No, he's just resting. It must be hard work to hatch." Sam touched the duckling's head lightly.

The duckling opened its eyes. They were like shiny black beads and gave its face a wise look. Its body stretched and heaved inside the rest of the shell.

"Come on," Sam cheered. "You can *do* it."

With an enormous shove of its legs, the duckling split the egg and plopped onto the grass in the can. It was a weak handful of dark, matted down, with feet like orange swim fins.

"He looks funny," said Rowen, "like he took a shower before he hatched."

Sam leaned close to the duckling. "You did it, baby! You made it!"

Rowen pointed. "Look, he's got all his parts."

The duckling closed its eyes again. Sam patted the bedraggled heap. "You know what—I'm going to call him Halloween. He's dark and orange, like Halloween colors, and he was brave enough to hatch in this spooky place."

Peep, peep.

The next egg was rocking in its can.

"Another one!" Rowen yelled.

They lifted the smooth, warm eggs to their ears one at a time. All seven were wobbling with inner activity.

"Sam," Rowen whispered. "This one's peeping inside. If you hold it against your cheek, you can feel tiny taps on the shell."

"This one, too," Sam said. "If I tap on the outside, the peeping gets louder inside. Rowen, we did it. They're *all* going to hatch."

Sam blinked. Tears of relief and joy stung the corners of his eyes. Embarrassed, he clung to the ladder and held an egg in front of his face.

Suddenly a bell dinged in the basement. The elevator doors rumbled open. Heavy footsteps clumped down the passageway.

DISCOVERED

"Mr. Hedges is back!" Rowen yelped. He dropped down the ladder to the cement floor. "Get down, Sam. Hurry! How could we have been so stupid?" Rowen looked at his watch. "It's ten past one . . . we're doomed."

"We can't leave Halloween," Sam cried. "He'll peep or fall out of his can, and Mr. Hedges will find him."

"Or Morton will," Rowen moaned. "I never thought about what to do *after* they hatched."

Carefully, Sam lifted the duckling from its can. He wrapped the bottom of his plaid shirt around the baby duck to make a pouch, then backed down the ladder. "Rosy and Rachel have one of those play ovens that heats up with a light bulb. We can hide him in there."

"They'll find him," Rowen said. "You said they find everything."

"I'll move the oven into my room. Maybe they won't notice it's missing," Sam said desperately. "Or . . . your grandfather! He has a toaster oven he uses to make cheese sandwiches. We could use that—"

"Are you nuts?"

They crept out of the boiler room and through the laundry room. Rowen grabbed Sam's arm when they reached the door to the passageway. "The minute he goes into his apartment, make a run for it," Rowen whispered.

Peep . . . cheep.

Sam peeked into the folds of his shirt and stroked the tiny lump. He could feel the duckling's heartbeat. Halloween looked up calmly, eyes alert. "If we hide him in the play oven, no one will find him—*no one.*"

Morton slipped through the doorway and circled Sam's feet. A low growl rumbled from his throat, and his whiskers twitched.

"Get away!" Sam said. "Shoo, scram—don't you dare come near him." He tried to push Morton away with his sneaker.

"Leave him alone!" Mr. Hedges loomed in the doorway. "Come here, you worthless cat," he said. He scooped Morton into his arms and rose stiffly. Mr. Hedges nodded toward the bulge in Sam's shirt. "Hand it over—*now.*"

"No." Sam shook his head and took a step backward. *"Never!"* he shouted.

Rowen's mouth dropped open in amazement. He stared at Sam.

"I'm not leaving him—*ever.*" Sam wanted to run. He wanted to take the duckling and hide. No one moved for a moment. Then slowly, silently, Sam lifted Halloween from his shirt and placed him on the superintendent's outstretched palm.

"What are you going to do with him?" Sam asked.

Mr. Hedges didn't answer. He stomped to the broom closet with Halloween in one hand and Morton squirming in the other. Mr. Hedges put the cat down and reached for a large cardboard box on the shelf, high above the sink. He placed the box on the floor.

"Please," Sam pleaded. "Don't put him where Morton can get—" He gasped when he looked into the box. It held strips of torn newspaper, scattered seeds, and a pan for water. What's going on? Sam wondered. Then suddenly he understood. "You knew!"

Mr. Hedges placed Halloween gently onto the paper nest and brushed past Sam. He gathered the remaining cans in several trips to the boiler and set them in the box, along with the old glass peanut-butter jar. "Water's getting low," he mumbled.

"He put it there!" Rowen and Sam said together. They slapped each other on the back and whooped loudly, while Mr. Hedges hung a light bulb above the box to keep the ducklings warm.

"You two make sure these ducklings stay *here,"* he said. "I've had enough floods lately to

last a lifetime. And I don't want any duck ponds being built upstairs." Mr. Hedges shooed Morton out of the broom closet and closed the door.

Sam stood still, listening to Halloween's lonely peeping. "We couldn't just leave the eggs in the park. Something happened to their mother and"—Sam's voice grew husky as he tried to explain—"the father duck left them, so they're . . ."

Mr. Hedges rubbed a broad hand over his head. Then he glanced at the clock on the wall. "They're fine," he said. "But you two are in trouble. You're both late for school. Clear out."

Rowen pulled Sam's sleeve and then bolted for the elevator.

"I'm going," Sam said, walking backward. "But the minute school's over, I'll be *back*." He turned and ran after Rowen.

• 10 •

RUFFLED FEATHERS

"What do you mean . . . *let them go?*" Sam was in the laundry room.

"You know what I mean," Mr. Hedges said from the doorway. "They're wild animals. They can't stay here forever. What kind of life would it be for them?"

"A *fine* one!" Sam declared. "They're warm and safe, and I can take care of them."

"You're here before breakfast and back the minute school's over," said Mr. Hedges quietly.

"It's Monday night, and you're in the basement. You even do the laundry, just so you can be down here."

"I like doing it. No one else has to take care of them. I don't *want* help."

Sam marched past Mr. Hedges and into the boiler room. Rowen was sitting on the floor, reading. The eight ducklings were in a chicken-wire pen behind him. Some stood in cereal bowls filled with grain. Some splashed in paint-roller pans full of water. Two huddled together, asleep under a warm lamp.

"How can you say that to him?" Rowen asked. "He's let the ducklings stay nearly two weeks, and he built their pen—"

"Shut up, Rowen."

Sam sat down beside him, breathing hard. He yanked a letter from his pocket and pressed it flat against his knee. "Can I borrow your pencil?"

Rowen nodded.

Sam tried to draw a duckling on the back of the blue envelope, but the lines kept blurring before his eyes. "Why don't they ever stand still?"

Sam crumpled the envelope and threw it into a dusty corner of the basement. Then he crossed to the pen.

Instantly, the ducklings charged forward. They stepped over each other and peeped frantically. Sam lifted Halloween from the top of the brown-and-yellow heap, then settled beside Rowen.

"Mr. Hedges is right," Rowen said slowly. "We should take them back to the park."

Halloween wobbled on Sam's chest. As Sam stroked him with a fingertip, the duckling closed his eyes. He sank like a slowly deflating balloon until he rested with his beak under Sam's chin.

"Ever notice the stripes by their eyes? They look like race cars—"

"Sam, *listen,*" Rowen said. "You aren't the only one in this building who cares about the ducklings. You aren't the only one who's helped them . . . and you know it."

Sam stood up, cradling Halloween, and moved to an old washtub filled with water. What's wrong with everyone in this place? he thought. Can't they see the ducklings are too small to go back? Halloween plopped eagerly onto the water. "We can't let them go," Sam said. "Not yet. They'll think we don't care about them any-more."

"Remember what it said in the library book?" Rowen asked. Sam kept his eyes on Halloween.

"It said," Rowen went on, "that mother ducks sometimes adopt orphaned ducklings. They'll mix them into their own broods—but *only* if the babies are small." Rowen joined Sam at the tub. "Once their down turns to feathers, it's too late."

Halloween paddled in circles on the water, then zoomed forward, leaving a ripply wake. Rowen got some food and sprinkled it around him. Halloween dove down and gobbled the sink-ing grain.

"Just *look* at him, Sam. He's ready to go. They all are," Rowen said and left the boiler room.

"Never," Sam murmured. He lifted Halloween, wriggling and dripping, from the tub and sat cross-legged on the floor.

Halloween stuck out two stubby brown-and-yellow wings and shook—from tail to head, knocking himself over backward on Sam's knee.

"Watch it, silly," Sam said, catching him. "What's the matter with you? Your tail looks kind of funny."

Sam bent down to look carefully.

A soft gray color was creeping into Halloween's down. Sam smoothed the duckling and rubbed him with his sleeve. Halloween felt rough and uneven under his fingers.

Sam's hands trembled. "It can't be," he whispered. But it was true. Feathers like tiny sticks were sprouting through the down.

"*How* can you have them already?" Sam asked quietly. "You still fit in my hands."

Sam held Halloween against his shirt until the duckling was dry.

THE DUCK
BRIGADE

The lobby was noisy the next Saturday. Rowen, Rachel, Rosy, Emily, Kasie, and Howard stood together, holding cardboard boxes. The boxes peeped and wobbled in their arms.

Sam stood by the front doors, staring through the glass. There was a box on the floor by his feet. His stomach ached with an empty feeling that wasn't hunger.

Mr. Hedges caught Sam by the sleeve. "Found this in the boiler room. I thought you might want it." He held out the crumpled blue envelope.

Sam jammed the letter into his pocket and picked up his box. "Come on," he called. "Let's go."

The duck brigade moved down the front stoop to Canal Street. Mr. Hedges followed with a bag of grain. They marched past the Fourth National Bank, the beauty shop, and the bakery. People on the street turned to watch. Then, finally, they reached the park.

By the lake, the children set their boxes down in the long grass and waited. "All right," Sam's voice croaked. "When we see a duck with babies the size of ours, I'll give the signal. And we'll let them go—together." He lifted Halloween into his arms.

Peep . . . peep . . . peeEEP . . .

Rosy and Rachel struggled to hold their ducklings. "Stop wiggling!" they ordered. Howard had a duckling under one arm and his binoculars around his neck.

Mr. Hedges sprinkled food along the shore, and ducks of different sizes drifted past. Then a speck-

led mallard came gliding from the reeds nearby, quacking steadily to the brood behind her. Her babies zigzagged over the water, chasing bugs and bobbing against each other. They were brown-and-yellow—and *just* the same size as the children's ducklings.

Sam buried his face in Halloween's soft down. "Be careful," he whispered to the duckling. "I'll love you no matter where you are." Then Sam knelt on the grass. "Ready?" he called.

Rowen, Emily, Rosy, Rachel, Howard, and Kasie held their wriggling ducklings over the water.

"Now!" Sam yelled. He gave Halloween a gentle toss onto the water.

The eight boiler-hatched babies hit the lake in one splashing rush. The mother duck swam in a slow, wide circle around them, quacking, then moved on. The ducklings surged after her, peeping and paddling in a long crooked line.

"She took them *all*," Kasie shouted.

Emily waved. "Bye, guys, we'll miss you."

Sam watched Halloween zoom toward a bug. "Did you see that? He got it!" Sam felt warm with

pride. But too soon it was hard to tell the ducklings apart.

Mr. Hedges put his hand on Sam's shoulder.
"Well, we'd better get these boxes back. We've
got some straightening up to do in the basement.
Morton's going to miss all that company."

"I know," said Sam with a sigh. He tugged the
crumpled envelope out of his pocket. Maybe I'll
be like my father, Sam thought. Loving from
long-distance. He smoothed the letter between
his hands. "I'm coming back here tomorrow to
draw a duck for my dad."

Rowen ran past Sam. "Let's go. Last one home
is a rotten egg!"

"Very *funny*," Sam called. He picked up Halloween's empty box and gazed at the ducklings
on the water. Then Sam raced Rowen home.